Oh Mycelium

Second Edition

By Sylvia Morrow

Cover by Unfortunate Reads

Content notes and description

This is a fantasy, paranormal romance story about two married women, one who is a pig shifter, falling in love with a genderless mushroom fairy who goes by they/them pronouns. It is an LGBT+ positive story and if that is not something you are comfortable with then this is not the story for you.

This story contains mushrooms, pigs, unusual genitalia, themes of potential rejection, adult romantic situations, arguments between spouses, unintentional misgendering, and more. The story is a standalone but would be best read with the rest of the series, if you ever have the chance and desire.

For information about additional content please reach out to the Sylvia Morrow website's content guide section or contact Sylvia Morrow on social media.

What Happens at the Gathering?

Oh Mycelium is part of a series of short books about small and unusual shifters, centered around a mysterious event called the Gathering. The final book in the series will take place there. Each book before that will be a standalone tale about how the shifters meet their mates, while the final book will simply be about the Gathering and the adventures they all have there together.

Chapter One

Sniff sniff.

There's something here, something that smells like truffles, but just a little bit different. Maybe it's a different variety, something especially delicious. I'm practically drooling at the thought. *Sniff sniff.* My snout wiggles up and down, searching the earth for that incredible, musky scent. It's getting stronger every second. My curly tail is even starting to wag a bit in excitement. *How embarrassing.* I'm not ashamed to be a pig shifter in the least, I only dislike looking so overly excited about something as silly as a fungus. Thankfully only Peggy, my wife, is here with me to see it.

"Oh, love, you must be onto something."

She laughs the brightest laugh and I remember the first time I heard her make that sound. I was walking through the town where many of us shifters lived, where we live now still. She was lost, looking for directions. When I stepped across the cobblestone street to give them to her, I could smell right away that she was my mate, the one person meant to be with me forever.

Pig shifters like me have very strong senses of smell, some of the best, so we're good at detecting that sort of thing immediately. Peggy was so perfect standing next to her wagon, looking entirely befuddled by the strange people in our town. Not all shifters can appear entirely human at all times, and she was a little confused by the occasional person with a feathered arm or scaled face. But I was only paying attention to her. To the fact that I had found my soulmate.

I got so excited, in fact, I *snorted* when trying to talk to her. She burst out in laughter, her eyes leaving the odd figures in the town to focus on me. She immediately apologized for laughing. I was so incredibly embarrassed, but she offered to buy me an ale as an apology, as well as thanks for the directions. The rest is history.

Now I turn my bristled body in a circle, our signal that I'm onto something, since I can't speak when I'm in shifted form, then continue moving along in the direction of that divine scent. *Sniff sniff sniff sniff*. The scent gets stronger and stronger until suddenly I see it: barely visible under some fallen leaves, a blue cap with white spots. It's not something I've ever seen before, so I'll have to be careful to make sure it's not poisonous, but for Sun's sake, it smells too good to pass up. I hurry toward it as fast as my short legs will take me, then push through the leaves with my snout, shoving them aside.

"Oh, would you look at that!" Peggy exclaims. "I've never seen anything like it. Be careful now, Donna."

I circle again to let her know I will be. *Sniff*. My snout is right up to the mushroom, nudging it, when *POOF*! A cloud of spores explodes into my face. I squeal and shake my head, stepping backward.

"Donna! Are you alright? Come here!" Peggy shouts frantically as I turn and run back to her. "Oh no, I hope that wasn't poisonous. Oh love, come on, let's get you out of here and to the doctor just in case."

I'm sure she's overreacting, but I'll go along with her anyway. You can't be too careful with fungi. There are too many types that can make you sick or worse.

We get back to the horse-drawn wagon and I shift into my human form. I'm coughing and I can feel spores in my nose. It feels like they're in my eyes and lungs. All over my face.

"Peggy, will you get me a wet cloth or something while I dress?" I ask.

I wash my face as best I can while we ride back, but it just doesn't feel like I can get the spores fully off me no matter how hard I try.

Once we're in town I visit the doctor, but he doesn't find anything wrong. He says to keep a watch, and we promise to do so. He's a good doctor, trained in science and magic, so I trust that he would tell me if I was ill. While the shifter town isn't large, we are blessed to have some excellent professionals, and our doctor is one of them.

Taking a long bath at home, I feel the need to drain the water and refill it twice while washing to get the spores off. But I still can't seem to feel clean. Peggy is such a sweetheart, and I don't want to worry her unnecessarily, so I don't mention my anxieties to her. She's already got so much on her plate. I use our special, homemade lavender-scented soap in my final soak to relax; no use worrying myself for no reason either.

Peggy and I are responsible for providing many of the specialty ingredients and food products for the upcoming shifter Gathering's feast. It's an important event for us and our partners. The *most* important event we have. The work we do for the Gathering pays for a large portion of our annual cost of living, and so I know she's quite stressed. I don't want to cause her any further anxiety with something likely to be entirely benign. I cuddle up to her in bed that night and kiss her dark brow.

"I love you. I'm sorry we didn't get any truffles today. Tomorrow I'll find double."

I grin at her in the pale moonlight coming through the window. She smiles back, her deep brown eyes wrinkling at the corners. The familiar minty scent of her toothpaste drifts to my nose as she sighs in mock disappointment.

"Yep, I'm going to work you hard. I should probably put you on a leash this time even. Naughty, naughty. Never listening to me about being careful. Such a bad, bad pig. A leash and a harness to guide you around like the naughty girl you are."

She tugs on my dark brown curls, and I offer her a gasp of faux outrage.

"You terrible woman. You're going to get me all riled up with your leash talk." My thighs press together involuntarily thinking of all the naughty games we used to play when we first got together.

I bite my lip and drag a finger down her full chest, which unfortunately for me is covered in her cotton nightgown. Her nipples harden under my touch. I think about continuing my stroking down past her rounded stomach to between her full thighs, until I feel a sneeze coming on. I turn and sneeze several times into my elbow. Those damn spores are still irritating me, I can feel them.

"Are you feeling ok, sweetie?" Peggy asks, brow wrinkling in concern.

She strokes my rosy cheek lovingly. Suns, I love this woman.

"I'm fine, darling. Just a tickle. Let's go to bed. Lots of work tomorrow."

I kiss her softly on her pillowy lips and we go to

sleep. I dream of the color blue and gentle caresses.

Chapter Two

Sniff sniff.

Back to work. I've found more than one truffle today, good-sized ones too. People don't understand how rare a high-quality truffle is and how difficult they are to find. There's a reason they're so expensive after all. *Sniff*...oh no. I pause when I smell the same scent from yesterday. I can't tell which direction it's coming from but it's strong. Musky, yet sweet, earthy. It's coming on suddenly as if it just popped up next to me. *That can't be right. I should have scented it from a distance.* I stop and sit, facing Peggy, our signal that something is wrong. She crouches in front of me.

"If we need to go back, let's leave, yeah? We'll go out tomorrow, somewhere else," Peggy says, scratching under my fuzzy chin where I like it the most.

I don't want to get hit in the face with spores again, but I also don't want to give up for the day. It's so early and we've had such a good time. Not only are there truffles around, but there have been tons of other foraging finds we'll be able to use in other goods, such as huckleberries and even golden raspberries. A day like today could be a huge boon for us. Looking around me, I don't immediately see that telltale hint of blue anywhere, so I stand. I circle around and cautiously step forward.

"Ok, if you say so," Peggy says warily and follows behind me.

It seems no matter where I go the scent of the blue mushroom stays equally distant from me. It's a wonderful day for foraging, probably the best day we've ever had, but I can't shake the uncomfortable feeling the scent is giving me; it's like I'm being followed.

It sounds silly to feel as if I'm being followed by a mushroom, I know, but I can't get the thought out of my head. It's like there are eyes on me everywhere. I keep expecting to turn around and see someone watching me, but when I look there's no one there, just Peggy picking berries or mapping out a particularly interesting location in her sketchbook for later reference.

Soon enough I can't handle the stress of it and decide to call it a day, claiming a headache so that we can head home. Peggy fusses over me the entire way, worried about my nonexistent headache, but I assure her there's nothing wrong, just exhaustion. By the time we arrive home, she promises to stop fussing over me if I go to bed early, so I agree. I could use some extra rest anyway; all that paranoia in the woods is getting to me.

We eat dinner early, Peggy's phenomenal mushroom risotto putting me in a brighter mood, and I tuck into bed for the night. She stays up for a bit, saying she has too much energy to sleep early and might as well start some pickling. She's always making jam or pickles or something; they're always delicious too. I was rail thin when I met her, unusual for a pig shifter, but I've put on plenty of weight since our marriage. Anyone would with daily access to her cooking. I nearly consider getting out of bed and going back down for a snack, but I know she'd deny me, tell me I should be resting. *Damn.* That's the price of faking a headache.

Sighing, I turn toward the window where the light is streaming in, and watch the clouds pass over the half-moon. Long, thin, tendril-like clouds pass over it. I lay still and watch them. They sway softly.

Those aren't clouds.

I sit up. There are no trees near that window with branches to blame. Those tendrils are too thin, too loosely flowing anyway. *What. Are. They?*

My heart races as I scoot farther back onto the bed, toward the bedroom door. I'm near the edge when suddenly *SMACK!* The tendrils slam into the glass of the window and stick there. Then more creep along the sides. And more. They begin crawling along the cracks, poking, and prodding. I want to shout for Peggy to run, to get away, but I'm frozen in fear.

Then the window begins to open; I must have left it unlocked.

The window opens halfway, and I begin to shake; it opens all the way and tears stream down my face. The tendrils slither along the inside of the wall, grabbing on, and begin to pull something up. Finally, *finally*, my body gives in and allows me to act. I scream just as a hint of blue appears above the windowsill.

"Peggy!" I scream, finally finding the ability to move my legs as I scramble out of bed. "Peggy, run! Go!"

My legs tangle in the cotton sheets when I try to step off the bed, and I fall, slamming my head on the floor.

For a moment I see stars and groan. I feel like I'm going to vomit from the pain of the hit, and I don't want to move. Then I see the shadow pass over the light on the floor and I remember what's happening. I scramble to my knees and crawl toward the door. I hear footsteps coming toward the room.

"Peggy no, don't come in, leave, run!" I scream, barely keeping my nausea from the head injury in check.

I'm nearly to the door when Peggy opens it, looking toward the opposite side of the room, the side with the window. Peggy's jaw drops; she's completely silent and still.

"Peggy?" I ask, voice trembling, as I wobbly stand, rising to meet her, to turn her around, but when I try to push her, she resists.

She just tilts her head to the side and furrows her brow in confusion, looking forward. She doesn't seem afraid.

"Peggy? Let's go."

She still doesn't move except to look at me.

"Honey," she finally replies. "Who's your guest?"

I swallow, then take a deep breath.

"I guess it's time to find out," I whisper.

Slowly, I turn around.

Chapter Three

When I first turn, I see nothing but the open window, the full moon perfectly centered in the frame. Everything is silent and I begin to wonder if it's all been a dream. I continue to turn, then see, sitting on my bed, a being unlike any I've ever seen before. My breath catches and I know now why Peggy took so long to respond to me; this creature is beautiful, breathtaking, and ethereal, but not something my brain can fully comprehend at first.

It takes me a moment to absorb everything I'm seeing before I'm able to breathe again. The being mostly looks human; two arms and legs, a face. Their legs are longer and thinner than a human's would be, their eyes are large like a doll's with long, curling lashes.

They remind me of a ball jointed doll I saw in the window of a shop that was far too expensive for Peggy and me. Porcelain and watercolor, stretched to strange but lovely proportions.

I step forward toward the creature, unable to stop myself, despite my rational mind telling me to back up. I reach out a hand and touch the softly glowing skin of their shoulder, then stroke their long, white locks. Reaching up to touch the blue cap on their head I pause, realizing it's no cap at all, but part of the creature's head itself.

The entire time I examine them the being just blinks their cobalt-blue eyes at me, watching silently. I lift their hand and stroke their long fingers, tipped with short, blue nails. I run my own hand along the small garment they're wearing, a simple shift that looks to be made of moss and leaves. Finally, I swallow my fear and approach the part of them that I'd been avoiding.

Shaking, I run my hand carefully along the inside of their arm where long tendrils are coming out. They close their eyes and sigh as their tendrils gently caress me in return. At first, I jerk my hand back, scared. The creature opens their eyes, tilts their head, and I see confusion, and maybe even a little hurt, on their sharp features. Oddly, I feel guilty about that, and so I gently place my hand back against their arm.

The tendrils slowly, tentatively, move against my hand in the same motion my hand moves against them. Then they begin to explore my skin, curling around my fingers, snaking up and down my wrist, at one point even flattening against my hand and sticking, then popping off, making me laugh. The creature jumps back at the sudden loudness of my laughter but calms down quickly when I apologize.

Taking a few deep breaths, I step back and shoot a glance toward Peggy, who is still in the doorway. She just stares at me with wide eyes. I shrug as if to say: *Fuck if I know what's going on.* I close my eyes, take one more deep breath, then open them.

"Hello. My name is Belladonna. This is my home. Who are you?" I manage to ask, surprised at my own confidence.

The creature blinks their large eyes back several times, opening and closing their mouth as if trying and failing to speak. I nearly interrupt before they clear their throat, then finally begin.

"I am called Azulene," they rasp out, their voice like crumpled paper and slow-moving water.

"Where did you come from and why are you here? I don't mean to be rude, but this is my bedroom, and you came in through my window in the middle of the night."

I gesture toward the open window, and they briefly glance toward it before returning their gaze to me.

"You found me in the forest and touched me, intending to take me. I enjoyed your touch and chose to follow you in my spores. Being near you proved to be acceptable, and therefore I decided to agree to stay with you. When I returned to my mortal form and made my way here, I found the opening to your dwelling over there and entered.

Should I have entered a different opening? That one seemed nearest to you." Azulene tilts their head in question. "Oh dear, it may take me a moment to remember the things I learned about this land."

"I still don't–" I begin, a hint of frustration entering my voice when I feel Peggy's hand on my shoulder.

"Why don't we take Azulene downstairs, get a warm beverage, and talk further, yeah? I think we have a lot to discuss, sweetie, and standing here in the doorway isn't the best place for it."

She looks at me with those compassionate eyes of hers and rubs her hand along my back in a comforting motion. I could never say no to her.

"I think that sounds good. Come along, Azulene." I wave my hand toward the doorway.

We walk downstairs and I check behind me as we go. They hold the railing and move slowly, as if they haven't used stairs much, but make it down fine. We go to the sitting room and choose separate chairs facing one another before Peggy goes to make tea. I sit in uncomfortable silence with Azulene the entire time she's gone.

Azulene watches me, blinking those huge doll eyes. I can't help noticing that though they're strange, they're also so handsome. Their long, curling, white lashes are a perfect frame for the unreadable swirl of emotion in those eyes. I want to touch their hair again; it felt like corn silk, quite like the tendrils on their arms.

They have tendrils on their thighs as well and I wonder if they feel like the other ones. I wonder if they can curl and grab and stick like the others. What it would feel like to be between those thighs. I shake my head, not liking where this line of thought is taking me. *I'm a married woman for Sun's sake.* I look at my clasped hands and think of work until Peggy comes back.

"Here's the tea then. Now, please be careful Azulene. It's very hot. I don't want you to get burned, alright? You may want to wait a moment before drinking it." Peggy sets Azulene's tea on the small table next to them.

Azulene nods, lowers their face next to the cup, and sniffs. They smile, their rosy lips wide. I can't help but to smile along. Their face has been so serious and flat the entire time and seeing them this way is such a surprise it catches me off guard. They bring up their arm and a tendril snakes into the tea just a tiny bit; it pulls back quickly. Azulene's eyes widen.

"Yes. Very hot."

They nod and sit straight, looking back and forth between Peggy and me before settling on me again. I clear my throat.

"So, I have some questions that may come off as rude. But, well, since you entered my home without permission, and have replied with some confusing responses, I am just going to be blunt."

I look at Peggy and find her frowning at me. She hates being impolite, but I don't like beating around the bush.

"First, what are you?" I ask.

Peggy gasps and seems to begin to object but I hold up my hand. This is an important question. There are dangerous beings out there and we must know what we're dealing with.

Azulene smiles. "I am a mushroom fairy."

I quickly blink several times. I didn't know such a thing existed. If one wasn't in front of me, I would have laughed at the thought. *Fairies*. My line of questioning continues.

"Alright. Why are you here?"

"You intended to take me. I followed you with my spores to decide if I wanted to join you. I decided I would go only if you came back to me. You did, but you did not find me again, so I decided to help you and come to you instead. I was worried you would not come back again if you could not find me the second time you were there. I tried to send out a scent to assure you I was still there, but you still did not come to my location.

"When you left without finding me, I knew I would have to come to you, to leave the forest. It's not a simple thing for my type to leave without permission. I had to pay a great price to the fairy ruler to take this form to get here."

Azulene looks very sad when they mention the great price, and something feels very heavy in my stomach. I don't want to ask but I feel obligated to.

"What do you mean, a great price?" I force out. *This is going to be bad; I know it.*

"I cannot go back to the forest. I cannot go back to the land of fairies either. I made the choice to be here with you. My home is here now." Azulene smiles.

There is sadness on their face despite the smile, but mostly hope. My stomach fills with dread. How do I tell this poor thing they've made the wrong choice?

"Where do you intend to stay? Do you have money? What do you eat? I don't know anything about fairies," I state firmly, hoping they perhaps get the point that they need to find accommodations. Instead, they just smile wider.

"I will stay here of course. We do not use money in the fairy lands, so I do not have any. I eat mainly plants and insects, but I could learn to eat other things, I think. I will have a lifetime to teach you both about fairies. I will marry both of you and love you forever. I already do. Love you, that is. I can feel it blooming inside me."

They look back and forth between us both,

excitement clear on their softly glowing face. Peggy's face seems to have lost all the blood as if she's about to faint. I reach over, grab her hand, and squeeze.

"You alright, darling?" I ask quietly.

She reaches a shaking hand over to grab her cup of tea and takes a sip, somehow managing not to spill.

"Fine, fine. Just concerned is all." She offers me a faux smile before turning back to Azulene. "We only have one bedroom, dear, so…"

"So, I'll sleep in your bed of course. I won't take up much space, I'm very thin," Azulene offers to us.

Peggy chokes on her second drink of tea.

"Azulene, that's not appropriate. We only just met you. If you choose to stay here, you may sleep on the sofa. I want to make it clear that Peggy and I are married and in a committed relationship. I'm sorry, Azulene, but we did not and do not intend to choose you as a mate. We will discuss this further at another time if you wish, but the fact remains that a mistake was made. Again, I'm sorry."

I can feel tears in the corners of my eyes. I shouldn't feel bad for this fairy that stalked me, broke into my home in the middle of the night, and is trying to force themselves into my marriage, yet somehow, I can't help it. Azulene's face falls.

"But it can't be a mistake. You were going to take

me. And you came back."

They look back and forth between Peggy and me frantically.

"We were going to eat you. We thought you were a regular mushroom," I say with a rough hitch at the end of my words from trying not to cry.

I know it's going to be hurtful, but they deserve the truth. They gasp.

"It can't be true. I can feel how different you are. You both are. I love you. I have given up everything to be here. Please."

Blue tears fall from the corners of their eyes. A sob breaks from Peggy's throat and she runs from the room.

"We will discuss this later. It's very late and we all need rest. There is a blanket on the sofa. Please get some sleep. Goodnight." I stand and walk away, heading to my bedroom.

As I walk up the stairs, I hear the keening of Azulene, and I break out into tears of my own.

Chapter Four

I didn't sleep at all. I held Peggy, who tossed and turned but did manage to sleep; she's always been one to get sleep where she can even in the toughest of times. I could hear Azulene crying most of the night. My heart broke for them early on, and I thought about going downstairs, but decided it wouldn't be fair to them; I didn't want to give them any false hope. At sunrise, I decide enough is enough and get up.

I descend the stairs with soft steps. It's quiet downstairs now. An hour or two ago Azulene had stopped crying, or at least stopped crying loudly. They're sound asleep when I creep by the sofa to check on them, and I see them curled up tightly. Their long legs are pulled up to their sharp chin, their tendrils wrapped around them like a blanket. I see the actual blanket still folded at the bottom of the sofa and I frown. *Did they not notice it?* I take the blanket and drape it over Azulene, careful not to wake them. Their clothes are so small and there is a chill in the air today. I don't want them to catch a cold, if their kind can even catch them; I don't know if they can, I suppose. Mushroom fairy biology isn't exactly something I studied in school.

I go to the kitchen, make myself some tea, and sit near the window, wondering what to do. Nothing seems right. The poor creature is homeless. They can't go out into the human world, that's for certain. People would do something horrible to them, I'm sure of it. *I wish Peggy was awake to hold me and give me a solution.* I rub my temples and set my head in my arms on the table. *What a mess.*

What I need to do is shift, get out of my head for a while. Being in my pig form lets me experience the world in a simpler way. I write a note for Peggy and leave out the back door. I won't go far, just into the backyard. We have a large yard for me to run about with lots of things to entertain my senses. It was our number two priority when finding a house to purchase, the number one being kitchen space of course. I undress and fold my clothes, set them by the door, and shiver in the cold before shifting into my porcine shape.

I am a medium-sized Berkshire breed. Humans don't appreciate the beauty of pigs and tend to think we're ugly and filthy and good for nothing but eating. It's awful really. Well, I think we're adorable and so does Peggy. That's all that matters.

My favorite apple tree, which has recently begun dropping fruit for the season, lies straight ahead of me. My tail wiggles in anticipation. I bite into a particularly juicy one and let the tart flavor wash away any worries I have. There are a few pleasant moments where the world is nothing but me, the crunching of fruit, and the crisp air. Things are simple, my mind is clear. Then I smell Azulene's delicious scent a second before I hear their voice.

"Mycelium helps trees grow strong, you know. In fact, that apple tree right there is benefitting from a symbiotic relationship with mycelium," they state in a near whisper.

I turn and look up. They're standing still, pigeon-toed, looking down at the roots of the apple tree. The tendrils on their body are swaying gently in the breeze. Some piece of knowledge clicks into place, and I move forward to nudge those threads with my snout. Azulene looks at me and smiles.

"I think you figured it out, didn't you? Those are my mycelium."

I circle, as I would with Peggy, before realizing my error. They giggle.

"You're a cute pig, you know? You look like you're wearing little white socks."

The pig part of me decides to embarrass me by flopping onto my side and squirming around, kicking my legs about, before rolling over and standing back up. A *squee* escapes into the morning air as my pig happily shows off, glad to be around someone who appreciates my form. The human me is nearly dying of embarrassment inside. Azulene continues to giggle and compliment my form as I trot to their side, planting my feet next to theirs to compare.

When I look down at their feet I snort in horror. Their feet are red with cold, and their legs are covered in goosebumps. I start toward the door and shift into my human form, grab my clothes, and head inside. As a shifter, I'm not particularly shy about nudity, and the look on Azulene's face when they see me is more curious than anything. *Good.* I'm glad to avoid awkward encounters.

"Come on." I wave to them to head inside. "You need warmer clothes."

When we both get inside Peggy is there waiting with tea and fruit.

"Darling, we need to find something to put them in. They're freezing," I tell her as I pull my nightdress over my head.

Peggy smiles slyly. I narrow my eyes at her suspicious look before she speaks.

"Oh, you're concerned about them, are you, love? I agree we should take care of them. Let's get them settled in, now."

She sets down her cup and takes Azulene by the arm, heading toward the stairs.

"Settled in? What do you mean by that?" I shout after her. "I just meant a robe or something!"

I sigh and stomp to the living room, flopping down onto the sofa where Azulene's blanket has been neatly folded once again. I fold my arms to my chest and pout, waiting for the both of them to return. Laughter drifts down from upstairs occasionally, making me feel grumpier. I start to wish I had gone up there, rather than sitting here alone. My eyes drift toward the blanket and something comes over me. Slowly, I lift the blanket to my face and inhale deeply. Azulene's scent is on it, that unique, incredible, indescribable scent. I can't help but rub my face on the blanket, the animal inside me wanting that scent everywhere. I don't even process what I'm doing; the part of my brain that should tell me to stop has been shoved into a closet for the moment. I moan and inhale again, then drag the blanket down my neck, to the place behind my ear where the mating scent is strongest.

My eyes fly open when I realize what I've done. *The mating scent.* The part of our body where we give off the scent that lets us know who our mate is. And here I am rubbing another person's scent all over it. I drop the blanket and scramble to get off the sofa, running into the kitchen. Grabbing a wet towel and soap, I proceed to wash my face and neck to get rid of any remaining trace of Azulene's scent. I know Peggy wouldn't be able to tell; humans don't have senses of smell strong enough to notice that. But someone else might. I would never want someone to think I was unfaithful to her. Peggy is my life. It would kill me to hurt her. It doesn't matter that Azulene is beautiful, intriguing, and divinely scented; Peggy and I have a marriage pact. We are mates. That's that.

I sit at the kitchen table and sip my tea, still warm, and then pop a perfectly ripe berry into my mouth. Azulene simply *cannot* stay here *and that's that*. I hear them and Peggy walk down the stairs. Soon they enter the kitchen.

"Sweetie, we've been chatting, and we think Azulene is going to stay for a while," Peggy announces in a bright and cheerful voice.

I drop the berry that I was about to put into my mouth in shock. She claps once and bounces on her toes.

"Anyway, look at Azulene, we've got them all dressed up! It took a bit to figure out how to get around their...mycelium? We did it though. Aren't they lovely?"

She steps aside and reveals Azulene, who had been hiding nervously behind her. My already open mouth drops further. In front of me is a beauty to equal my wife. My face burns with guilt for even thinking it, but I can't help the truth of it. They've been put in a loose, white, sleeveless dress. An old blue shawl is draped over their shoulders and blue stockings are on their feet. Peggy added some necklaces that fall beautifully against their flat chest and bracelets that fit right where their tendrils end. They lift their arms and spin, a nervous look on their face. The shawl looks like wings in the morning light. I can see how they are something magical. They stop and face me, biting a lip that has been glossed with shiny pink color.

"What do you think?" they whisper.

I close my mouth and clear my throat.

"It's fine. Good," I nod to their feet. "You need shoes."

I try not to let how strongly I'm feeling show; I don't want them to think I want them to stay. Or want them in any way. They nod and blush.

"Peggy tried but none of them fit. She said we would go to a shop tomorrow. We do not wear shoes where I come from, so I did not have any. I'm sorry. I have a lot of things to get used to, I guess."

"That's fine, we'll teach you everything," Peggy tells them with a pat on the back.

I clench my jaw and narrow my eyes at Peggy. I can't believe she's doing this. While she's always been the generous and kind type, she's hardly been the kind to make some sort of decision this big without me. I can't imagine any married couple just deciding to let someone move in with them when only one of the people agrees. The more I think about it the more upset I get. Suddenly, tears spring up in my eyes. I stand up and head toward the stairs.

"I have some things I need to do today, alone. You two clearly have things you need to do as well. I'll see you tonight," I bite out.

I head upstairs and dress quickly, leaving the house as soon as I'm done. Peggy tries to speak with me at one point, but I brush her off. If I try to discuss things with her in the mood I'm in, things will not turn out well.

I walk a long way, until I reach the edge of the forest, and then undress and run wild in my pig form for hours. I nap in the sunlight, enjoying the solitude and carefree moments before I must get dressed and begin the walk back to town.

Once I reach the bustling town square, I decide to take the busier street home, as it's beginning to get dark, and I don't want to get caught alone just in case. There are some nasty and cruel humans out there in the world. There aren't many who are fully aware of this shifter town as far as we know. Peggy finding it was a fluke. But if the day comes when they discover it, we need to be ready. Most humans don't even know we exist but many of the ones that do hate us. We must remain always vigilant.

I walk past the antique shop and see my friend Tom, the owner, closing up, his ginger-haired husband Philip next to him. I smile; they're a wonderful couple. I remember when they first met.

The two bird shifters were only teens when they scented each other mid-flight over the town square. They crashed, landing right next to Mrs. Sweets, the porcupine shifter who is running the Gathering. No one could forget that moment.

A lovely woman takes Philip by the freckled hand, stands on her toes, and kisses him full on the mouth. I pause in shock. Next, Tom reaches over and kisses Philip, then leans down to do the same with the woman. I shake my head. *Tom and Philip are mates*. And that woman is *a human*, I can smell her from here. Tom turns and sees me, then smiles and waves. I wave back.

"Donna!" Philip is waving now. "Come over and meet our new mate! She's even better than Tom!"

Tom snaps his head to the side to look at Philip. Philip just laughs.

"Ok, ok, I love them the same but come meet her anyway!"

They both roll their eyes at him, but they do so with smiles on their lips. I don't hesitate to join them; I've known the men since they were boys and they're good people.

"Hello, you scamp," I say to Philip, playfully slapping him on the shoulder. "Always the troublemaker. And Tom cursed to deal with him."

I bow my head solemnly in Tom's direction. Tom

returns my nod, his smooth, dark hair only barely disturbed by the motion.

"It is a curse indeed," he says as Philip feigns outrage. "However, a blessing as well, as he has brought the lovely Jasmine into our lives. Have you met Jasmine, Donna?"

Tom places a broad hand on the lower back of the woman next to him and nods toward her.

"I have not. A pleasure to meet you," I say as we shake hands. "And may I ask how you all know one another?"

All three look at each other with wide smiles before Jasmine speaks.

"Well, it turns out I'm their mate. It's rare, apparently, but here we are!"

She bounces on her toes and takes a hand from each of the men in each of hers. My mind spins. I know there are multiple-mate families; there are many in town. It's just that seeing a couple of shifters that I knew were monogamous, and so deeply in love, accepting someone of an entirely different species into their relationship so easily… well, it's a bit on the nose, isn't it?

"Are you alright, Donna?" Tom asks.

I realize I'd been standing silently.

"Oh, I'm sorry. I just have a lot on my mind today and was reminded of something. I'm fine though. And I'm ridiculously happy for you all." I take Jasmine by her hands and look her in the eyes. "These are good men. Take care of them and they'll take care of you."

She smiles wide and a frizzy curl flops in front of her eyes.

"Don't worry, I will. They need me. I've got them covered."

She attempts to blow the curl out of her eyes, but it flips back into place. Philip pushes it back so that it stays out of her eyes.

"We've got each other covered," he says as he tickles her sides.

She laughs and we all follow suit. We talk for a few more minutes and then I make my way home.

I have a lot to think about and more to talk to Peggy about. And I must talk to Azulene eventually too, I suppose. Only I just don't know what I'm going to say. Or what I'm going to do. For Sun's sake, do I even know anything?

Chapter Five

I arrive home and hear more giggling from the kitchen. *Damn it. They really do get along well.* Sighing, I head toward the warm light.

Entering the kitchen, the first thing I notice is the smell. My stomach rumbles at the familiar spicy, sweet scent. I look down at the table and see a plate of gooey cinnamon rolls, dripping with warm icing. My mouth instantly begins to water. I look for Peggy and Azulene and find them leaning against the counter. Both are wearing aprons dusted with flour and sugar and all sorts of other ingredients. They look like the sweaty, glowing picture of those who've spent hours in the kitchen baking. It's a good look on both of them.

"Welcome home, sweetie," Peggy tells me in her most seductive voice.

"Hello, darling." I narrow my eyes at her. Seems I'm doing a lot of that this past day, but she keeps acting as if she's scheming behind my back. She knows the best way to seduce me is food. What is she planning?

"I'm teaching Azulene how to bake. Isn't that wonderful? Won't you love having two bakers in the house? Then I'll teach them how to cook your favorite dinners. You'll get to eat all the best things every single day."

She slides a finger down her glistening cleavage as she speaks, leaning against the counter in a way as to pop out her full hip and show off the curve of her waist. I growl quietly. She must know exactly what she's doing to me. Even over the scent of the treats, I can smell her pheromones. She's trying to seduce me, and I don't know why. *Azulene is right there!*

I turn to focus on Azulene and then notice, really notice, Azulene's appearance now. They're biting their lip and looking at me with those huge eyes, half-lidded. They look every bit the handsome rogue under the apron they're wearing, in a sleeveless button-up shirt, tight black trousers that are slit in the thighs to allow for freedom of their tendrils, and boots reaching to their knees. They lean back against the counter and prop one leg against the bottom cupboard, and lean their head back, revealing the full stretch of their neck and the flat planes of their torso. I wonder what it would be like to slide down that plane. Azulene's delicious scent hits me then, strong, but this time there is an extra layer to it, a layer of desire.

Between the scents of the two people in my house I'm throbbing between my legs and my mind is racing. *What is happening? Am I dreaming?* I step toward Peggy, ready to tear her clothes off before starting on Azulene, just before a shred of sanity makes me step back. A question rises to the top of my mind.

"What were you doing?" I stop dead still and ask.

"Baking," Peggy responds immediately.

I shake my head.

"No. You were done baking by the time I arrived. I mean right before I came in. You were giggling and you both smell like pheromones. What were you doing?"

I look between the two of them and wait. Peggy's grin falters for just a second and now I step toward her. I sniff her neck, right behind the ear. I smell Azulene on her, but I don't smell kisses. The scent is only faint, so likely just a hug or a gentle touch. That it's there at all makes me feel a little angry, but she didn't cheat, so that's a relief.

"No, I didn't cheat if that's what you're thinking," Peggy spits out, stepping away from me with a furious look on her face. "You should know me better than that, but you should also know that Azulene feels just as destined for us as you were for me. We knew we were meant to be together within the first moment we laid eyes on one another. Because it was *destiny*. We trusted it, yeah? Why can't we trust *this* too when it's clearly meant to be?"

She pulls off her apron and tosses it on the counter.

"It's fast, yeah, but you had me in your bedroom the first night we met and moved in within a week and I'm not even a paranormal like you. Why are you being like this then?"

She turns to Azulene, who now has tears in their big eyes. "Come on, now. I'll help you run a bath. It's been a long day."

She takes Azulene by the hand and they leave me alone in the kitchen, where I begin to cry. I sit in the chair, lay my head on the table, and cry for a long time. I cry until my tears run dry, wipe my face on my shirt, and get myself a glass of water. Standing at the sink and looking out into the night, I wonder what tomorrow will bring. I sit back at the table and bite into a cinnamon roll, groaning in delight. They're fantastic. Peggy has always been a good teacher and I'm sure Azulene will be baking this well on their own soon enough. *If they stay*. I lick my fingers clean and stand. It's time for my own bath now. Dirt doesn't stay away just because of emotional turmoil.

Azulene is already asleep on the sofa when I pass by. Upstairs the bedroom door is closed, so rather than stop in to grab pajamas first I just get a towel from the linen closet and head straight to the bathroom. The tub has been scrubbed clean already, thankfully, so I fill it up and get right in. I add some relaxing lavender soap to get some bubbles and lay back, letting the heat soak my worries away, even if it's just temporary.

I'm so relaxed that I'm nearly asleep when I'm startled by the soft click of the door handle turning. I look to see Peggy closing it behind her. She's in her green silk robe, the one that looks so bright against her umber skin. It's my absolute favorite. Her makeup is washed clean for the day, and she looks so fresh, so youthful. Neither of us are young girls anymore but when she's like this you'd hardly know it. One side of her mouth lifts in a half smile.

"Hello, Donna. Sorry to interrupt, I just want to speak to you alone and I figured I can trap you when you're at your most relaxed." She chuckles lightly.

I snort back at her.

"How devious. Have a seat then and say your piece."

I pat the edge of the tub, she sits. Her robe falls open just a bit, revealing her smooth thigh and my breath catches. I stroke her gently with one wet finger, making her sigh. I can smell her interest and I lick my lips. She slides my hand away.

"No funny business, love. We need to talk."

She cups my jaw and looks seriously at me. I roll my eyes and nod, laying back under the bubbles.

"Go on, then," I grump.

"They're going to stay with us because they're innocent, they have nowhere else to go, and because we're not cruel. Maybe they'll stay for a little while; maybe forever. We will decide, but we'll decide *together*. I'm not going to force you into accepting them. I love you and, no matter what, I want you. I chose to mate with you. We went through the ceremony at the Gathering, made our promise, and we're not going to break it. Do you believe me?"

Her eyes search mine for an answer.

"Yes. Your honesty is one of the things I love the most about you," I reply.

It takes no hesitation; if she says she chooses me then it's true. She relaxes.

"Good. Now, I need you to also know that I desire Azulene," she states plainly.

My jaw clenches. I knew that, yet hearing it stated so bluntly hurts.

"You certainly didn't take long to decide that. You've barely met them and you're willing to harm our marriage," I grind out from between my teeth.

"You know you do as well. I wouldn't mention it if you didn't. I can see the way you look at them. It's the same way you look at me; like you're starving and I'm dinner. You forget what the Gathering ceremony does to humans, how it changes us. I can sense this connection. No, it's not a bond like shifter's have, but it's something else. Maybe it's a fairy thing, I don't know, but you won't even try to find out. Why? Why won't you accept that if we both want them then it might be ok to try?" she pleads.

I finally snap and splash my hands against the water.

"Because if it doesn't work, I could lose you. It's so soon. Why risk you on someone I've just met? I wouldn't risk you on someone I've known a thousand years. You might fall for them and forget about me. I'm older now and I'm just a forager. Your assistant, at that. I'm plain. They're a magnificent, unique being. I'll forever be worried you'll want them over me. That's it, ok?"

Tears spill over my cheeks. It's embarrassing to admit being envious, being afraid. I've never been that type. Peggy's features soften.

"I already told you that you'd never lose me. And anyway, you don't think I have enough room in my heart to love more than one person? Donna, you're so different from Azulene there's no choosing one or the other. You both being so different is a positive, not a negative. And for Sun's sake why are you listing those things about yourself as if they're bad? Where do I even start? Just my assistant? Excuse me? I couldn't even do the work I do without the ingredients we find together. And once we get back here you do all the financial work and logistics that I know nothing about. You think that's not important?

"And you're worried about being older? I talked to Azulene and they're hundreds of years old. You didn't even ask them their age. And *PLAIN*? You're the most beautiful woman in the world to me. Did you forget we're fated mates, yeah? The beings bound to be more attracted to one another than any other beings?

"I understand you're frightened sweetie, and I won't rush you, but I promise you have nothing to worry about. I will always love you." She takes my face between both of her hands and kisses me softly, reassuringly, several times in a row.

I reach up and stroke my hand along her jaw, behind her ear, down her throat. She sighs onto my lips and kisses me harder, pressing into the seam of my lips with her tongue. I open for her, letting our tongues glide languidly together. One of her hands smooths back my hair while the other begins to trail down my neck, my chest. Her thumb sinks just below the water to where my peaked nipple is waiting, gently grazing it. I whimper into her mouth.

"So sensitive," she purrs; I shiver.

Her mouth moves down to lick behind my ear and nip my earlobe while she continues to rub and pinch my nipples. She knows this drives me crazy.

"Peggy," I pant out, my breathing rapid now. "I need you."

I throw my arms around her, not caring that they're dripping wet. Her green robe gets drenched when I pull her down against me. She moans as she pulls away from me.

"Then you'll have me, darling."

She smirks as she undoes her robe, revealing her entirely nude body underneath. The naughty woman knew she could have me tonight.

"Get in here already," I whine.

She complies, sinking into the water before me. I wrap my legs and arms around her, kissing her with an intensity we've missed for a while.

"I love you," spills from my mouth with every breath.

I kiss, lick, gently bite, every inch of neck and chest, worshiping her like the goddess she is. She grabs my ass and pulls me tighter against her, feeling the core of me slippery against her stomach even in the warm water. She slides a finger along the back of my thigh, then up the inside, stroking my inner lips. I whimper.

"Yes. Please," I beg and grind against her hand.

She laughs softly into my ear, making me shiver, as she slowly inserts one, then two fingers inside me.

"My dear wife, so easy to please. So eager to feel me inside her sweet cunt," she whispers against my neck.

I groan, moving up and down as she curls her fingers rhythmically. She sucks on my neck in my favorite spot right as she brings her thumb against my clit, making me buck against her.

"Fuck," I yelp.

She chuckles, moving faster inside me, inserting a third finger, caressing the most sensitive spot, and moving her thumb faster. I kiss her hard and cry out as my whole body tightens, my cunt clenching around her fingers, as I come hard and strong.

"Yes, Donna, yes, just like that, come for me. So beautiful. Sun's sake, Donna, you're magnificent," she whispers against my neck when my head falls backward.

Soon, she starts to slow, and I come down from the orgasm. My peak has been reached but now I'm starving for her. I kiss her and glide my hands up the inside of her thick thighs, spreading them as wide as they can go in this tub. I throb again just at the thought of touching her but right before I can reach her core, she places her hands on top of mine.

"Not tonight, Donna. Just you. Ok? I just want you to hold me. Let's go to bed. Just love me tonight."

She reaches back up and pushes my wet curls behind my ears. I don't really understand, and I'm disappointed to say the least, but there is a vulnerable look in her eyes that tells me not to challenge her. I nod.

"Alright. But I want to be big spoon."

I tug on one of her black braids and she laughs loudly.

"That's more than fine. I think I need to be the little spoon tonight anyway. You're perfect for me as usual, sweetie."

She kisses my forehead and takes my hands. We stand and grab towels, then dry each other off, giggling like girls. We get to the bedroom, dress in cotton nightgowns, and sleep comfortably the whole night. My wife is perfect, and no matter what comes between us, we will always find a way to work things out.

Chapter Six

In the morning, I wake to the sounds of a busy kitchen and the scent of maple syrup. My stomach rumbles. The other side of the bed is cold but that's not unusual; Peggy is the early riser in this marriage. After dressing I head downstairs, finding Azulene in the kitchen with my wife. They're both standing at the stove, Peggy instructing Azulene on how to make the pancakes. There are quite a few black and tan colored flat things on a plate on the counter that appear to be mistakes made during learning. I chuckle; they look better than my first attempts. Peggy turns, sees me at the entrance to the kitchen, and smiles.

"Well, hello there, sleepyhead. We're just about to finish the pancakes. Azulene and I are getting them down now. And they've squeezed fresh juice. Have a seat."

She turns back to the stove and flips one of the cakes. Azulene waves a hello and I wave back, smiling. When they see my smile, they smile back, their eyes lighting up. I feel a bit guilty about last night, but today is a new day and I decide we'll start over. There will be time to discuss all of that though after breakfast. This little piggy is hungry. I sit, and soon the others join me. Plates are filled and we all start eating.

"This is great," I say between bites. "You're going to make a great cook, Azulene. Peggy will teach you well."

I smile at them, hoping they get the hint: that I'm telling them they're welcome to stay for now, that I'm apologizing in my way. I don't like saying sorry, I'm stubborn, but I do want them to know that they're welcome...for now, anyway. Their large eyes light up, so I know they understand. I relax my shoulders and take a bite of pancake. It really is good. After a few minutes of casual conversation, I realize how late in the morning it's getting. The Gathering is not far off and there is still much to do.

"Peggy, we need to work today." I turn to Azulene. "Will you be joining us in the forest? We could use any help we can get."

I pat their shoulder but pause when I see the crushed look on their face; I pull my hand back.

"What's wrong? What did I say?"

They lower their head to stare at their hands, wringing them, their long fingers tangling together.

"I can't go back, remember? I can't leave here. Ever." They look up into my eyes. "I can stay in town with people but that's it. Humans or shifters. No forests, no fairies. I chose to leave my old life behind."

Real understanding of their sacrifice dawns on me for the first time. We're truly all they have. My throat tightens up.

They look back down at their hands. They whisper, "I told you."

Silence fills the kitchen. We sit for a long moment. I knew what they said before, but it hadn't really hit me, why Peggy has been pushing so hard for us to let them stay here whether I accept them as a mate or not, how serious this situation really is. *They really can't go home*. After this I really need to work on better listening to my wife. I clear my throat.

"Alright then. We will find a job for you at the house while Peggy and I go to the forest. If you're going to be staying with us you need to contribute to the household then, alright?"

I pat their shoulder again and smile. They look up at me, worry still on their face.

"Are you sure? There's not much I know how to do yet," they say, still quietly.

I scoff.

"We'll find something. Do you want to be part of this household or not?"

I'm stepping out of my comfort zone now. Peggy takes a deep breath, and I can see her biting her lip. Her face is glowing, and her eyes are lit up. Azulene's eyes flick up to mine and open wide.

"Yes, I do, absolutely," they rush out.

"Then we'll figure something out. No layabouts allowed."

I rub my hand along their upper arm in what I mean to be a friendly, familiar gesture but I forget about their tendrils. When I graze them Azulene's mouth falls open and a soft moan escapes, their eyelids briefly flickering. I yank my hand back and set it in my lap. They turn and stare at their plate.

"I should get cleaned up, I'm covered in flour," they stutter out before getting up and stumbling out of the room.

Their scent trails behind them and it takes a heavy load of strength for me not to moan when I smell it. The scent of my own desire fills the room and Peggy's mouth lifts in a smirk.

"Don't even start," I groan at her before resting my head on my arms. "That's what I get for being kind."

"Don't be a brat because I'm right." Peggy retorts.

She sits down next to me.

"Come on, you glum bum. It's time to get to work."

We give Azulene some simple household tasks: folding laundry, washing dishes, things like that. They seem more than happy to do the chores and I'm more than happy not to do them. Peggy and I set off to a place we haven't been to in a while, a particularly secluded area that could be fruitful this time of year. We get to an isolated spot that I sense could be a good starting point but before I shift, I decide to have a talk with Peggy while we're alone.

"Honey, if you want to be intimate with Azulene I'll allow it, but I don't want you to forget me. I'll die without you."

I spit out the words as quickly as I can. I thought it over and decided that if there is some sort of connection, something like a mate bond happening, it's not within my rights to stop it for her; I must trust Peggy. I've always trusted her, and I can't stop now. Peggy drops her bag, a shocked look on her face.

"Sweetie, what in Sun's name would make you think I'd ever forget you? Or that I could ever live without you? Being with someone else would only be an addition, there would be no subtraction required."

She wraps her arms around me and holds me tightly, rubbing her hands up and down my back.

"I would never, ever give you up for anything in the world."

I rest my head on her shoulder. If she says it, I believe it. I'll always believe her.

"Will you be with them then? Azulene?" I whisper.

There is silence for a moment.

"Yes," she finally replies. "You will too. You just have to stop denying it."

I sigh and begin to undress.

"Maybe. I want to get to know them. I don't think that's all too strange, to want to get to know the one who is turning my life upside down, is it?"

I glare sideways at Peggy before I shift into my pig form. Peggy laughs loudly.

"No, I think that's fine, little piggy. We have all the time in the world. What we are short on, however, is time to get ready for the Gathering, so let's get going. Find us some truffles, yeah?"

She scratches my chin and I snort in appreciation. Here we go again.

Sniff, sniff.

We work in the forest all day, bringing home an excellent haul. Peggy gets right to work processing everything we found while I head upstairs to clean myself up. I meet Azulene on the way, as they are folding towels and placing them in the hall linen closet.

"Hello, Azulene! How was your day?" I stop to ask.

They pause in their work, clutching a towel to their chest.

"Oh, it was fine. I cleaned up and weeded the garden. A woman named Sarah stopped by but said she would see you another time. Nothing else happened. I think I am going to run out of things to do very soon, honestly."

They chuckle softly. The way they tilt their head to the side every time they laugh causes their white hair to fall in a shimmering wave over their glowing shoulder. It makes me want to stroke those many strands, but I resist the urge, just barely.

"We'll find more for you to do soon, I promise. Once we start putting everything together for the Gathering, things will be insanely busy around here and we will be very glad to have you around, believe me."

I take the towel out of their arms and put it into the closet for them, brushing against those long fingers as I do so.

"And speaking of the Gathering, we will need to take you to see Mrs. Sweets as soon as possible if you'd like to go." I pause. "Would you like to go?"

Their eyes open wide.

"Yes, I would love to. Do they allow fairies to go? We are not mates."

Their eyes drop to the floor and their shoulders slump. Shit. I didn't think about that. *I'll figure it out*.

"Don't worry. You're part of our family either way."

I lift their chin with a finger until their eyes are aligned with mine.

"Don't forget that. Whatever happens."

I didn't realize I felt that way, that I now consider them family, but I guess I do. Well then, it's time to treat them that way.

Chapter Seven

The next day I take Azulene out to get a job. Something part time and simple; the world is still overwhelming for them, but they can't just sit inside doing nothing. I take them to my friend Sarah. When Azulene mentioned Sarah stopping by it reminded me that she owed me a favor.

"Sarah, hello, I know you need some extra help and I have someone for you. Say hello to Azulene, your new part-time employee."

I gently push a terrified Azulene in front of me. Sarah shakes her head in confusion and drops the laundry she'd been folding.

"Well, good day to you too, Belladonna. Always a pleasure." She barks out a laugh and smooths back her sweaty red hair. "Pleasure meeting you, Azulene. If you can do laundry, then you can get to work."

"Good to meet you, ma'am. I can do laundry just fine. Should I start today?"

Azulene beams at me and wrings their hands nervously.

"Might as well. Gloves and aprons in the back. Get

them on and meet me back up here. Glad to have a new man to help me. Or is it woman?"

"Neither. Both. Other?"

Azulene shifts back and forth on their feet, their cheeks turning red.

"Ah, no matter to me. Let's get going then!"

Sarah smiles and gestures for Azulene to head to the back room.

Azulene breathes a sigh of relief and waves goodbye to me. I return the wave then start back home, a proud smile on my face. I'm so glad for them; nervous, hopeful, but glad. After I get Peggy, we then head back out to forage for the day.

"Do you think they're going to be alright?" I ask Peggy on our way out.

"They'll be more than alright, love. They're going to thrive. Just wait and see. I doubt they're going to be doing laundry forever, but whatever they do they'll be fine because they'll be coming home to us."

She kisses me on the cheek, and I rest my head on her shoulder for the rest of the trip. In the late afternoon we pick Azulene up on our way home. They are sweaty and tired, but they have a huge smile plastered across their face. They practically skip to the wagon, and once seated, they bounce in their seat the whole way back excitedly telling us about their day.

"There was a man who brought in twelve tiny sweaters. He said they were for his children. I said I was surprised he had twelve babies, but he said they were adults. He was so offended. Apparently, they are guinea pig shifters. How was I supposed to know? Why would they need sweaters anyway, they have fur!"

Azulene has the most comically incredulous expression on their face, and I can't help but grin.

"Well, everyone loves to get dressed up. Speaking of which, we're visiting Mrs. Sweets tomorrow to get you an outfit for the Gathering. If you thought the guinea pig man was crabby just wait until you meet her."

I raise my eyebrows and smile at Peggy, who just sighs. Mrs. Sweets really is quite prickly.

"Are you really sure she'll let me go there?" Azulene bites their lip.

"I'll make sure of it." I grab their hand and squeeze, stroking the back of it with my thumb, allowing myself the luxury of the coolness of their skin for just a moment before releasing it.

They make dinner that night with Peggy. They seem to be a very quick learner, every task they're given performed well within a couple of tries. I comment on how smart they are, and they blush.

"I have wonderful teachers," they say in that raspy

voice I am coming to find quite charming.

I realize more and more how much it sounds less like crumpling paper and more like crunching leaves. I smile into my salad as I take my next bite. Autumn has always been my favorite season.

"Sarah seemed to think you performed quite well and was grateful for the help. The day after tomorrow will you go back?" I ask.

"Oh, yes!" they reply. "Sarah is great, and the job was more fun than I anticipated. Plus, I need something to do."

"Good! She'll be glad to see you. Much happier than Mrs. Sweets, I will warn you." I scrunch up my face in apology. "But like I said, I'll deal with her." I nod then, more confident than I feel.

"Alright." They sink in their seat a little.

Peggy rubs a hand on their back to comfort them.

"Don't worry, we've got this," she says.

I know she's right; even if I fail, Peggy will fix it, I'm sure.

"Nothing to be afraid of then. Old Mrs. Sweets and her vampire husband will accept our family as is, no buts about it."

I set my fork down next to my empty plate and look at Azulene to see their already white face blanch further at the mention of Mrs. Sweets' vampire husband. I laugh. He tends to have that effect but he's the nicer of the couple. We won't see him in the daytime anyway.

"Thank you for dinner, you two. I'm going to head to bed early. You should get rest too. It's a long ride."

The ride *is* long, so we start out early in the morning, traveling a long way through the woods to get to the Sweets' home. When we finally arrive, it's already early afternoon and the place is bustling with people. The Gathering isn't far away and there are people bringing all sorts of things in now. There are an exceptionally large number of people dying fabrics in vats spaced all throughout the property. There are so many colors out drying it's like a rainbow. Mrs. Sweets isn't only in charge of overseeing the event but she's in charge of ensuring everyone is wearing the proper garments. Anyone previously at a Gathering already has their official attire so Peggy and I are covered; Azulene, however, is not. They will soon likely have their own color hanging out to dry.

I spot Mrs. Sweets with her spiky light blonde hair and pinched face looking over some beads that were just delivered.

"Mrs. Sweets!" I rush over to her, making sure to get to her before anyone else can steal her attention away. "I have someone very important for you to meet."

Her nose wrinkles and her eyes squint.

"I hope it's not another person for me to dress. I've already got people throwing new mates into the mix last minute left and right. Ridiculous year." She stomps toward Peggy, who is standing by the cart. Azulene is nowhere to be seen. "Well, where is this person, hmm? I don't have time for games."

Peggy coughs and looks behind her. When no one shows up Mrs. Sweets growls.

"Azulene, now," Peggy shouts over her shoulder.

I hear rustling and see Azulene's blue cap pop up over the side of the wagon. Rising to their full height, Azulene finally waves awkwardly, then steps around to stand next to Peggy. My wife nudges them in the side.

"Oh."

They blush all over, more nervous than I have ever seen them.

"Hello Mrs. Sweets. I am Azulene."

Mrs. Sweets looks them up and down for a long moment before speaking.

"And what exactly are you, hmm? You know this is a shifter event, yes? Not just for any riffraff that wanders into town." She waves her hand dismissively.

Azulene scoots a little behind Peggy.

"I am a mushroom fairy," they stutter out.

I begin to explain that they are here as part of our family, but Mrs. Sweets cuts me off before I can begin.

"So, what do you want with me? You aren't a mate. You aren't a shifter. I certainly don't want some cast off fairy at my event. Fairies are always trouble anyway, and if you are exiled, I can only imagine what a mess you are. So, I ask again, what do you want from me, hmm? I'm a busy woman so get it out, cast off fairy," she spits out.

I look at Azulene and see blue tears starting to fall from their eyes. Oh, hell no.

"They are our mate, you just assumed they aren't. I just didn't have a chance to explain. We're here to get a garment made for them for the mating ceremony," I snap at Mrs. Sweets and watch her mouth pinch even further than I thought possible.

I hear Peggy make a choking noise and Azulene gasp, but my eyes remain locked on Mrs. Sweets.

"You should have said so sooner. How annoying. Follow me. Fairy mates, ugh."

She begins to stomp toward the house. We all gape at one another for a moment before slowly following along. Azulene stares at me the whole walk to the house, wide-eyed, nearly tripping several times. My throat bobs and I stare ahead, trying not to panic. Oh, what did I do?

Chapter Eight

We say as little as possible during our time at Mrs. Sweets' house and are silent nearly the entire trip home. Everyone has a shocked, yet contemplative, look and I think we all just need time to think over what the hell I just got us into.

We arrive home and all sit down in the living room facing one another, looking everywhere but in each other's eyes. I fuss with a loose thread on the hem of my shirt while I watch Azulene's tendrils explore the spaces in between the sofa cushions. Peggy clears her throat and both Azulene and I startle.

"Well, I think it's time to talk then, yeah?" Peggy announces. "Donna, you not only made the choice for all of us but announced it as well, so why don't you speak first, since you're so good at it."

Her tone is cold and my face burns in anger.

"How dare you be upset?" I spit out, suddenly switching from feeling awkward to enraged as I stand. "This whole time I've had no choice. I've been told I must accept this triad. Finally, I do, even if it was just to defend Azulene's honor, and now I'm told I'm wrong. Well, I won't have it. You've wanted this and now you've got it."

Azulene shoots up from their spot on the sofa, glowing brightly.

"This is not what I wanted," they shout.

I step back, my calves hitting the chair behind me and nearly knocking me down. They rarely ever speak above a whisper; to hear them shout is surreal.

"I do not want defense or pity. I want you. I want you both and I want you to *want* me back. That is what I want."

Their eyes turn downward, and they sink back onto the sofa. They place their head onto their hands and begin to cry. Peggy rushes over and wraps her arms around Azulene, trying to calm them down. I sit and breathe for one moment, then two.

"But I do want you," I say quietly. "I just don't want to *have to* want you. And I don't want having you to mean losing Peggy. That's all."

I return to pulling at the thread on the hem of my shirt. There. I've said all I can say. The room is quiet. A cool hand takes hold of mine.

"I am sorry that I took that choice from you. If I could change things I would. I hope you believe me. I would like to spend my life making it up to you if you will let me. And I swear to you I will do everything I can to keep Peggy with us because I care for her just as much as I care for you. All three of us together is my desire. Please let me prove it."

I breathe in Azulene's scent as they speak, letting it fill me up without fighting it, or trying to analyze it, for once. I let it mingle with Peggy's scent still in the air. The two mix perfectly.

"Alright then," I whisper and lift Azulene's hand to my mouth.

I softly kiss their warm palm and they shudder lightly; I turn their hand and kiss the cool backside of it, kiss each fingertip, and at the end they moan softly. I look across to Peggy to see her breathing heavily, her eyes focused on my lips. I return my focus to Azulene and begin to kiss up the inside of their wrist, then their forearm. Their breathing speeds up as they intently watch my every move. They take their other long-fingered hand and run it through my soft hair, and I sigh. I lick the inner corner of their elbow and they jump a little, surprised. We both chuckle. I start to lick toward the base of their tendrils, but they gently pull me back by my hair to stop me. I look up at them in confusion.

"That's very sensitive," they pant out. They trail off and their face goes red, "It's…"

It takes me a moment before it clicks.

"It's an erogenous zone? As in, it will sexually excite you if I stimulate you there?" I ask.

Their face goes even redder. "Yes, exactly."

I sink to my knees in front of them, run my hands along the outside of their thighs, then the tops of them.

"Here I thought that's what I was intending to do. Sexually excite you, that is. Unless you don't want me to."

I begin to slowly, very slowly spread their legs apart. The wider apart they get the more tendrils can move freely. They're moving chaotically now, every which way.

"Is that what you want? To be…" I sink low enough that my head is right in between their thighs. "…stimulated?"

"Suns yes," they nearly growl as their tendrils latch onto the sides of my face, pulling me closer.

I hear Peggy gasp and I throb between my legs at the thought of her watching. I allow myself to be tugged further in, while I run my thumbs along the base of the tendrils as I go. Azulene moans through their teeth and several of their thickest tendrils work themselves into the sides of my mouth, pulling it open.

I stare up into Azulene's wide, worshiping eyes, with my mouth held wide open, their tentacles grabbing my tongue, exploring the insides of my cheeks, nearly gagging me by dipping into the back of my throat. The sensation is so bizarre but from the way Azulene is panting, and from the strength of the scent coming off them, I can tell that they are enjoying it quite a lot. I decide to try and find out what else they might like, and with some effort, I close my mouth and suck gently on the tendrils. Their eyelids flutter and their hips roll. *Good.* I suck hard, taking the tendrils deeper and licking their base with my tongue. Their eyes roll back, and they bury their hands in my hair.

"Oh, Donna, yes."

They rock their hips and moan while I lick and suck, their tendrils exploring and gripping chaotically on and off the entire time, for several moments, before finally they pull me off them and lift my face to theirs.

"Belladonna, my destiny, we need to go upstairs, all of us. Let us be together."

They stroke my cheek, that is wet with saliva and tender from being sucked on by their greedy mycelium, and I nod eagerly. There's nothing I want more than to include Peggy in this.

We stand and I skip to Peggy, wrapping my arms around her, kissing her hard. Peggy kisses me in return, her nipples hard against me from how much she was enjoying watching Azulene and I. I take Peggy's hand, then Azulene's, and we run up the stairs, giggling the whole way.

When we get to the bedroom, we all jump into the bed and the laughter soon morphs into the sounds of passion. Azulene kisses Peggy, who sighs dreamily. I reach around to the front of Peggy's shirt and unbutton it while she's kissing Azulene. I unbutton her pants and slip them off her. She's left in only her undergarments, and I stand and gaze appreciatively for a moment before beginning to remove my own clothing.

By the time I'm done undressing, Azulene has already freed Peggy's breasts from her camisole and is licking her nipples. I never thought I'd find the sight of someone else licking my wife attractive, but here we are.

Azulene is the only one fully clothed, so I approach them cautiously. I want to make sure I have consent each step of the way, so when I touch the first button on their shirt, I make sure to pause in case of a no. When I don't receive one, I unbutton it and move down one. I keep going until their shirt is off. I do the same slow routine with their pants. Soon they're in their undergarments as well. Their long, thin limbs wrap around my curvaceous wife, and I smile at the contrast.

Peggy looks over to me and says breathlessly, "Come here now and kiss me, little piggy."

I roll my eyes at the nickname but follow her command gladly, kissing her soft mouth while

Azulene kisses down her breasts, her stomach, her hips. Peggy's kisses become more frantic the farther down Azulene goes, until finally Azulene begins to remove Peggy's underpants. She breaks the kiss.

"Oh, Azulene, what are you doing?" Peggy pants out.

I kiss my favorite spot behind her ear and inhale her scent.

"What do you think I'm doing, Peggy?" Azulene grins. "I'm going to thank you for being so kind to me."

Azulene slowly drags Peggy's panties the rest of the way off her body and tosses them onto the floor. They spread her legs wide, and I can't help but pause my kisses to watch what's about to happen.

Azulene kisses up Peggy's inner thigh until they reach her core. They slip one finger inside my wife while their tendrils tickle along her outer labia. I lose sight of the details when Azulene leans in and begins to lick and suck on her clit, though I can see the tendrils moving rhythmically along with the slow pumping of their hand.

Peggy pants and moans, grabbing my hands. I lean in and kiss her fiercely, feel her shuddering as Azulene works her faster and harder. I let go of Peggy's mouth and move to her breasts, sucking her nipples and nipping them in time with Azulene's movements. Soon I feel Peggy begin to stiffen.

She squeezes my hands tightly and cries out in a powerful orgasm. I watch her with awe as she shouts *"Yes, yes,"* to the ceiling. She's so beautiful. Her glistening skin takes on a golden sheen in the fall moonlight, her full lips swollen and purple from kisses. She starts to come down from the orgasm and I kiss her softly again.

Azulene pulls away from Peggy and I turn to them. I crawl to Azulene and use my momentum to push them backward, straddling them. I lean down and kiss them frantically, tasting my wife's delicious cunt on their mouth. I groan and grind myself against the crotch of Azulene's undergarments. I'm not sure what to expect under there, it hasn't been my business to ask, but now I'm determined to find out. I need to feel them, to taste them, to fuck them however I can.

I kiss down Azulene's neck, tugging down the undershirt they're wearing as I go. I'm surprised to find that they are entirely smooth underneath; they have pectoral muscles, yes, but no nipples. I cock my head to the side briefly but then smile. Interesting. I kiss their chest and their stomach, making them giggle; I look up at them when they laugh.

"Sorry," they say. "Ticklish."

"I'm absolutely using that against you in the future," I tell them with a wicked grin.

One of their tendrils smacks me on my behind and

I yelp.

"You deserved that," laughs Peggy.

I roll my eyes and kiss the side of Azulene's hip, where their underwear band starts. I slip my fingers underneath and slowly begin to pull down. Their cheeks turn bright red, and they start chewing on their bottom lip. I make it a couple inches down before they stop me.

"Wait," they say. "Just so you remember, I am not human. Or shifter. I have a different anatomy. Do not be upset."

They look afraid, and so I lay a gentle kiss on one of their hip bones and smile.

"I know you aren't human and I'm looking forward to exploring every bit of you. You too, right, Peggy?"

I look over at my wife and smile. She returns the grin and nods, biting her lip seductively.

"Looking forward to it very much."

We grin at each other before I turn back to Azulene, who has now lost the look of fear. I trail a finger along the bases of the tendrils at their thigh, making them shudder.

"How I love making you shiver like that. Let's see what else I can make you do."

I take their undergarments and drag them off their body, spread their legs for them. My eyes widen in surprise and, at first, confusion. It takes me a bit to realize what I'm looking at; I know it's something I've seen before, but I can't place what. I move closer, sliding my hands along their tendril-coated thighs as I go, making them whimper. When I get close it dawns on me what it is I'm seeing: *gills*. Not like a fish has gills, but how a mushroom has gills. *Makes sense.* I realize I have no idea what to do and don't want to hurt them. Communication has always been a problem with us before this; now seems as good a time as any to attempt to fix that, I guess.

"You'll have to instruct me a little, dear."

I run the very tip of my finger softly across the folds of their gills. They gasp and shut their eyes, nodding.

"I am...I am sensitive there. Be soft at first."

They open their eyes and run their luminescent hand down the side of my cheek. I kiss their thigh again and nod.

"Yes, my dear," I whisper right against their apex, and they whimper, their tendrils tightening their hold on me.

I softly run just the barest kiss of my lips against them and listen to them hum as they tense. I stick out my tongue just slightly, running it along one rib of their core, and they writhe. I flatten my tongue and they moan and push against my mouth. *There we go.*

Peggy places an arm under Azulene's head and lifts them, bringing their faces together into a crashing kiss. I lick against the outside of Azulene increasingly firmly, faster. A long, whining sound escapes their mouth from between the kiss and Peggy and I both groan in unison at how fucking sexy it is. Azulene's hips buck when I slide my tongue in between their folds. The folds are surprisingly shallow and taste like sweet earth; I hum at the unique but not unpleasant taste and their strong reaction to my act.

Azulene breaks away from the kiss as their tentacles pull my face away suddenly. They run their fingers through my hair over and over.

"Donna, Donna," they say my name like a prayer over and over until their breathing slows. "I just need to warn you that my…reproductive organs are there. You are going to make me…you know."

Their cheeks turn bright red.

"Are you saying you're going to orgasm? Because that's the point, Azulene."

I raise my eyebrow and grin.

"Well, yes, but I will…oh Suns it is embarrassing."

They release my hair and cover their eyes. They attempt to close their legs, but I push my body between and move up. Holding their chest tightly, I kiss their neck.

"You can tell us anything, love," Peggy says against the other side of their neck.

Azulene is quiet for a long moment but then nods.

"Spores."

They quiet again after that one word. Peggy and I look at one another.

"Spores?" Peggy asks.

"Spores." Azulene nods.

"Is that all?" I reply. "You've already spored me once." I laugh against their neck. "I'd be honored to receive them again."

A terrifying thought hits me.

"I'm not going to get pregnant with little mushroom babies, am I?" I sit up for a second. I absolutely do not want to carry children.

Azulene grabs me and pulls me back down, their face shocked.

"No, oh no, not unless I use my specialized tendrils to insert them into your cervix when you are fertile. Or you could impregnate me when a different specialized tendril extracts one of your eggs… actually this is a long conversation maybe we should have another time. Either way, I promise we are safe now."

Peggy and I both raise our eyebrows. *Well, that is*

definitely a conversation to have at some point. I nod.

"Another time then. But for now..." I slide a hand down their body until I am nearly where their thighs meet. "I want to get back to less talk, more action."

Azulene giggles and the sound sets my heart fluttering. *How I could have ever denied these feelings, I'll never know*. Their tendrils wrap around my waist and tug me down. I yelp and laugh as I'm dragged lower. When I reach the sweet spot, I immediately dive in without hesitation, causing a long moan to come from Azulene. They grab Peggy and pull her down next to them, kissing her neck and chest, sucking on her full breasts, as I lap between their gills.

I feel a slithering feeling coming up the back of my thighs, to my hips, and soon my panties are roughly tugged down. I gasp onto Azulene right as a group of their thickest tentacles slip into me, writhing around, plunging in and out, the feeling unlike anything I could have ever imagined. The writhing mass inside caresses every inch of me. My actions falter as another thin tendril finds a way to lock around my clit and stroke it as if it were the tiniest cock. My brain can't process the sensations all happening at once and I grab tightly onto the blankets next to Azulene's thighs to try to ground myself. I groan as they work faster inside me and out, inserting more and more, and I break apart, my eyes rolling back as I shout their name.

When I begin to come down, I immediately return to my work on Azulene with even more vigor than before, using both my mouth and hands to lick, kiss, stroke. Their thighs clench tightly around my head; their tendrils lock on me everywhere. I can feel a vibration low in their pelvis and suddenly a soft cloud of spores puff into my face. It takes everything I have in me not to sneeze, the only thing keeping me from doing so is the sound of Azulene moaning my name and the deliciously vulgar feeling of their tendrils dragging down my dripping cunt.

Chapter Nine

We cuddle up together and just breathe, after Azulene bashfully wipes the light dusting of pale blue spores off my face. They insisted I won't get some sort of asthma attack or lung infection after I sat up in panic and asked. It would be quite embarrassing to try to find a doctor to clear up a lung fungus that came from my mate's…not sure what to call it, actually.

"Azulene, what do I call your…" I playfully walk my fingers down their stomach, but they grab my hand and yelp.

"Ah! No! No more embarrassing questions for me tonight, please." They bury their head under a pillow and Peggy and I both laugh. They whine, "Stop laughing, it is not funny."

I try to stop but when they peek one of those huge, blue eyes out to look at us I crack up anew. After a moment Azulene starts laughing too and we all wrap ourselves up into one big silly, giggling cuddle.

The next few days are spent more lying about and romancing one another than working. I gobble up every bit of information I can about Azulene, trying to make up for the days I rejected them. Though my mate declaration was not initially meant to be real, I have found that I am happier I made it each moment I spend with Azulene.

I am not afraid for my relationship with Peggy; if anything, this seems to have restrengthened our bond. Being reminded of how important communication is to our relationship, and how nothing can change our love for one another, just brings us closer. It also doesn't hurt that watching her be intimate with Azulene is surprisingly intoxicating.

Azulene is fitted for their Gathering garment by a disgruntled Mrs. Sweets. The garment they are given is in a color that matches the one to be worn by Peggy and me and I must admit they fit in perfectly with the two of us. We make a strange but wonderful trio.

Every night after we are done with our work for the day, we make sure to sit together at the kitchen table and have an open line of communication. After what we went through those first few days, we learned that communication is the most important thing for us if this relationship is going to work out. Airing any grievances, sharing any struggles, admitting worries, all those things are done at the table if they're not done during the day. It's worked wonderfully so far; having this honesty, openness, and trust is everything I could want. I've been able to learn so much about Azulene, and even things about Peggy I'd have never known otherwise. I feel so blessed to have met this strange and wonderful creature.

"Azulene, are you sure you don't have any worries about the Gathering tomorrow?" I ask, sipping the mint tea they prepared for us all.

Azulene slips a tendril around my forearm and squeezes, a smile on their face.

"I do not worry about much of anything anymore, not now that I have you two."

I snuggle up against them and sigh happily. It may have been strange and scary at first, but this mushroom grew on me.

Peggy Bonus Chapter

"Go ahead, little piggy. I'm going to grab that one on the tree way up there. Meet you in a sec."

There's a massive mushroom that'll fetch us a good price on the trunk of a big, old tree. Problem is, it's pretty far up. I can get it, but it'll take some climbing. That's alright though, I can do it. I may be middle aged, but that doesn't mean I'm out of shape.

Donna scurries ahead in her pig form. We're looking for fruit mostly today, but this fungal treasure is just too good for me to pass up. I climb the tree quickly and easily, many years of practice under my belt. Ever since I was big enough to reach the lowest branches, I've been climbing trees. I always feel a little bit better surrounded by the forest.

I guess I've always loved the freedom of nature. That's why I'm a forager. I couldn't stand working in a shop all day, I need to move around. The ability to up and leave was always so important to me. Used to be, anyway.

Before I met Donna, I never let myself be attached to anything or anyone at all. I was always traveling. In fact, I was traveling when I met her. I shouldn't have been able to even enter the shifter town. There are wards to prevent unknown humans from entering. But I got in. And I thank the Sun every day that I did.

I may not travel as much these days, but I still get to be in the woods, and now I have a companion with me when I go. Someone I'll never tire of. And when I return home, I have two perfect people there with me. My life is fantastic.

When I cut down the mushroom, I place it carefully into the large sack I have with me and swing it across my back. When I make sure the weight is distributed correctly, I prepare myself for the trip downwards. But then, something in the leaves shifts.

"Hello, Margaret. Oh, they call you Peggy, do they not?" A voice comes from the leaves. Apples fall onto the branch in front of me and into a pile that vaguely resembles a face. Eyes open. A mouth. "Have you thought about what I said?"

My lips close tightly, forming a thin line. This *thing* won't leave me alone.

"Yeah, you can back off then, right? I told you I'm never going to leave them. It's pointless for you to keep coming around here. You fairies banished Azulene, you can't have them back. They're our family now." I begin to climb swiftly down the tree. The apples fall as I go, a distorted face forming with them as I do. "Go on then. Back to where you came from. I've got work to do."

"You are going to regret taking them in. It is only a matter of time," the apple fairy rasps out.

"Yeah, well, I'll worry about it then, yeah? Have a good day then. I'm off." I jump off the last branch and walk away, hiding my shaking hands in my pockets.

Snort!

"Oh, hello there Donna," I say as I crouch down to scratch my wife's bristly chin. "Find anything good?"

Donna circles around and takes off in the direction opposite the tree I was just on. Thank the Sun for that. Jogging happily behind her, I let the warm sunlight soothe the cold that had taken over my blood during the conversation with the apple fairy.

Later on, at home, I make sure to stew up a pot of applesauce with a satisfied smirk on my face.

"You are looking cheerful tonight," Azulene notices as they sit at the kitchen table.

"I'm feeling great," I say as I spoon applesauce into their dish. Gazing into the pot of the boiled and mashed fruit I grin with satisfaction. "Just thinking."

"About what?" Donna asks.

I spoon the last of the apple sauce into her dish. "About how nothing will ever come between us."

Azulene Bonus Chapter

A few weeks after Donna and Peggy accepted me into their lives, I sit at the base of the apple tree in our backyard and help it grow stronger and healthier. It's one of Donna's favorite things and I want to make sure it's always here for her. I'm not a tree fairy, so it's not as if I can make apples bloom in winter or anything, but I can help nourish the roots and nudge things in the right direction. It may not be huge, but if it's something I can do for Peggy and Donna, I will do it.

I stand and shake off the soil that has gotten on me, then wrap my mycelium around my arms and legs. Adjusting my cloak, I prepare to exit the yard and make my way toward town to meet Peggy at the bakery where she is negotiating the sale of some of the jam we've been working on. I nearly make it to the gate when suddenly a figure steps out of the bushes.

No, not out of the bushes; the figure is the bushes.

I sigh. I had hoped never to see them again.

The ruler of the fairy lands.

"Hello, Azulene," they say in our native tongue. It feels strange to hear it again, though it has not been that long. "Have you reconsidered my proposal?"

I clench my jaw and ball my hands into fists. This is not someone I want to see. For the last two weeks they have been visiting me every few days; I cannot seem to get rid of them.

"I have. My answer is the same. I will not marry you and I have no interest in returning to the fairy lands. I made my home here when you exiled me, and I am happy. Please let me be. My answer will not change." I answer them in the human language, even though my mouth craves to use the language of my previous home. I simply want to show them I am part of this world now and this is one way. The glow of my skin flares in exasperation. "If you insist on bothering me with this then I will ask you to leave and not return."

"Tsk. So rude to your ruler," they admonish me. They shake their leafy green mane and wag a finger of polished wood. "You would give up a seat on the throne for a life down here with, what? A human and a pig? Down in the filth and the dirt when you could be in a place of pure magic? Are you a fool?"

"I like the dirt and I love my wives; this place has a magic of its own. Maybe I am a fool, but I am free. I have made my choice, and it is here. Goodbye."

I open the gate and walk past them, their green eyes squinting at me as I go by. I hope I don't hear from them again but there's a good chance I will. It doesn't matter anyway; my answer will never change. I will never leave. I make my way to the town square to meet Peggy and Donna. When I see them together, I light up, literally. My skin glows brighter and I can barely control my mycelium. I jog to them and wrap my arms around them.

"What's gotten into you, sweetie?" Peggy asks with a laugh, twirling me around.

When we pause our twirl, I kiss her cheek and grin.

"Just so happy to have you is all. Both of you. I would not trade you for anything."

"Well, I might trade you both for some of those cinnamon rolls I had a few days ago so maybe we should make some more to prevent that," Donna says with a cheeky grin.

I roll my eyes at her.

"By 'we should' you mean 'Peggy and Azulene should', right?" I ask.

"You know me so well," she replies. She kisses me

and smiles. "You love me, you know it."

I sigh. "I do. I really do. Oh mycelium, I really do."

Dedication

Thank you to Vera, Latrexa, Evan, Luka, Owyn, Ryan, Sarah, Tawny, and all the other writers and artists who have encouraged me to keep writing. I wouldn't have kept going without you.

Special thanks to Wolfgang and Aubrieta for giving me some much-needed advice and encouragement on this particular story. And thank you to Tiera and Desaray for the help with getting the second edition released.